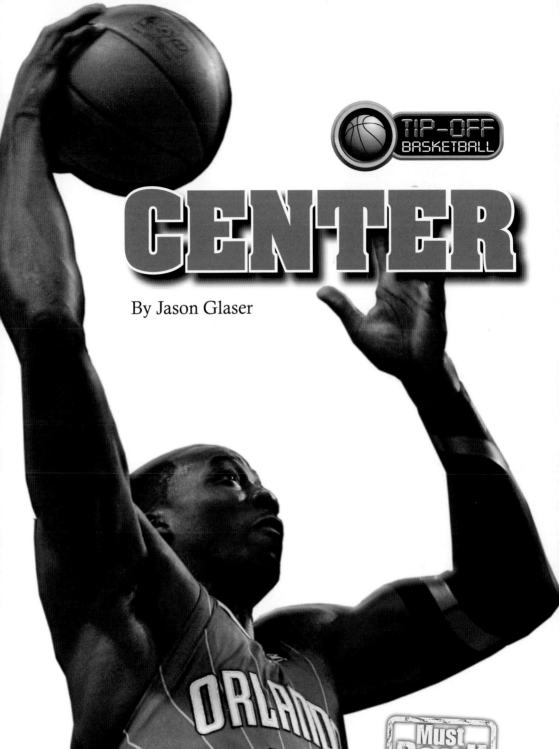

TIP-OFF BASKETBALL

CENTER

By Jason Glaser

Must Read!

Gareth Stevens
Publishing

Please visit our Web site, www.garethstevens.com. For a free color catalog of all our
high-quality books, call toll free 1-800-542-2595 or fax 1-877-542-2596.

Library of Congress Cataloging-in-Publication Data

Glaser, Jason.
Center / Jason Glaser.
   p. cm. — (Tip-off, basketball)
Includes index.
ISBN 978-1-4339-3972-3 (pbk.)
ISBN 978-1-4339-3973-0 (6-pack)
ISBN 978-1-4339-3971-6 (library binding)
1. Center play (Basketball) I. Title.
GV887.74.G53 2011
796.323'2—dc22

                              2010018765

First Edition

Published in 2011 by
Gareth Stevens Publishing
111 East 14th Street, Suite 349
New York, NY 10003

Designer: Michael J. Flynn
Editor: Greg Roza

Gareth Stevens Publishing would like to thank consultant Stephen Hayn, men's basketball coach at
Dowling College, for his guidance in writing this book.

Photo credits: Cover, pp. 1, 39 Elsa/Getty Images; cover, back cover, pp. 2–3, 5, 7, 8, 12, 19, 25, 27, 33,
35, 38–39, 44–48 (basketball court background on all), 19, 22–23, 29–31, 43 (basketball border on all)
Shutterstock.com; p. 4 Garrett Ellwood/NBAE/Getty Images; p. 5 Noren Trotman/NBAE/Getty Images;
p. 6 Hulton Archive/Getty Images; p. 7 Gjon Mili/Time & Life Pictures/Getty Images; p. 8 Superstock/
Getty Images; p. 10 NBA Photos/NBAE/Getty Images; p. 11 (Russell) Dick Raphael/NBAE/Getty Images;
p. 11 (trophy) Jesse D. Garrabrant/NBAE/Getty Images; p. 12 Wen Roberts/AFP/Getty Images;
p. 13 Mike Powell/Getty Images; pp. 14, 37 Brian Bahr/Getty Images; p. 15 Rick Stewart/Getty Images;
p. 17 Jeyhoun Allebaugh/NBAE/Getty Images; p. 18 Sam Forencich/NBAE/Getty Images;
p. 19 Noah Graham/NBAE/Getty Images; p. 20 Ron Hoskins/NBAE/Getty Images;
p. 21 Andrew D. Bernstein/NBAE/Getty Images; p. 22 Brian Babineau/NBAE/Getty Images;
p. 23 Barry Gossage/NBAE/Getty Images; p. 24 Al Bello/Getty Images; pp. 25, 32 Layne Murdoch/
NBAE/Getty Images; p. 26 Harry How/Getty Images; p. 27 Christian Petersen/Getty Images;
pp. 28, 33 Ronald Martinez/Getty Images; pp. 29, 31 Steve Babineau/NBAE/Getty Images;
p. 30 David Liam Kyle/NBAE/Getty Images; p. 34 Doug Pensinger/Getty Images;
p. 35 John W. McDonough/Sports Illustrated/Getty Images; p. 36 Kevin C. Cox/Getty Images;
p. 38 Jed Jacobsohn/Getty Images; p. 40 Chris Cole/The Image Bank/Getty Images;
p. 41 Alex Martin Photographers/Getty Images; p. 42 Imagemore Co., Ltd/Getty Images;
p. 43 Inti St Clair/Digital Vision/Getty Images; p. 44 Gregory Shamus/Getty Images;
p. 45 Focus On Sport/Getty Images.

CPSIA compliance information: Batch #CS10GS: For further information contact Gareth Stevens, New York, New York at 1-800-542-2595.

CONTENTS

Boldface words appear in the glossary.

Big Men, Big Plays

The center is usually the tallest player on a basketball team. Towering above the other players, centers use their height and quick hands to grab balls out of the air and slam them through the hoop. Centers are usually the players who stand out on **offense** as well as **defense**.

Shaquille O'Neal

Standing Tall

In 2002, the Los Angeles Lakers were going for their third **NBA** championship in 3 years. Not only did the New Jersey Nets need to find a way to stop the great Lakers shooting guard, Kobe Bryant, but they also needed to stop the Lakers' powerful center, Shaquille O'Neal.

As the Nets guarded Bryant, O'Neal **rebounded**, shot, and **dunked** for 100 points in a four-game sweep. He made another 45 points from **free throws** as the Nets **fouled** him to keep him from shooting. On June 12, 2002, the Lakers became NBA champions. Shaquille O'Neal was named the Most Valuable Player (MVP) of the finals for the third straight year.

As the name suggests, centers are in the middle of the action. Read on to learn how centers come up big for their teams.

The NBA Finals is a best-of-seven series. The Lakers beat the Nets four games to none to win the 2002 finals!

Kobe Bryant

Shaquille O'Neal

When Dr. James Naismith invented the game of basketball in 1891, the center was probably the most important position on the team. Today, centers go up high and get the ball, but not the way Naismith imagined.

James
Naismith

The Tip-Off

One thing that's remained the same throughout the history of basketball is the tip-off. Every basketball game from the very first one has started the same way. A center from each team jumps up for a ball tossed into the air by an official. Each center tries to "tip" the ball toward his teammates to gain control of play.

Center Jumps

Back in Dr. Naismith's time, the beginning of the game wasn't the only time centers jumped for the ball. In the original rules, a "jump ball" took place after every **field goal** and free throw as well. A center who could jump high gave his team a better chance of starting with the ball, even if that team had just scored.

Two centers reach for the ball during a game in 1948.

Jump balls both slowed down the game and favored the team with the tallest centers. In the 1930s, basketball games stopped having jump balls after baskets and free throws. Today, the NBA uses a jump ball at the beginning of the game—which is called the tip-off—and when possession can't be decided due to fouls on both teams or when two players are wrestling for the ball. The NBA is one of the few leagues that still use jump balls other than for the tip-off.

Dr. James Naismith, who died in 1939, didn't like the rule changes that removed jump balls from the game. In his opinion, the changes ruined his original idea for the game of basketball.

Lines on a basketball court mark an area near the basket that players can be in for only a short while. This area, known as the free-throw lane or key, was once just 6 feet wide. Big centers easily scored and defended the net from the key. Centers crashed into each other jumping around the key. In the 1950s, the lane was doubled in width to keep tall players in check and keep them from hurting each other.

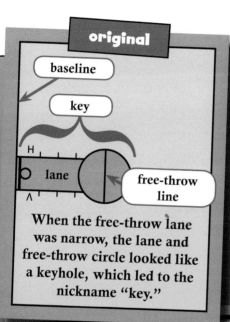

original

baseline

key

lane

free-throw line

When the free-throw lane was narrow, the lane and free-throw circle looked like a keyhole, which led to the nickname "key."

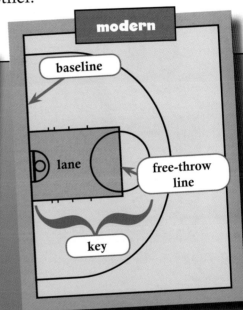

modern

baseline

lane

free-throw line

key

Lanes, Keys, and Paint

The free-throw lane, or lane, is the area between the baseline and the free-throw line. Players in this area are said to be "in the paint" because the floor is often painted a different color. The free-throw lane is sometimes called the "key." The top of the free-throw circle, which is called the "top of the key," is a popular shooting area.

George
Mikan

Throughout the years, many of the biggest men in basketball worked to define the center position with their outstanding play. Let's take a look at some of the biggest big men in the game's history.

The Rule Changer

George Mikan was so good he caused rules to change. The rule that widened the key was often called the "Mikan Rule" because it was meant to slow him down. The **shot clock** was added after one team passed the ball around for almost an entire game rather than let Mikan have it. His masterful blocking and rebounding, paired with his unstoppable **hook shot**, made him the first modern center.

Mikan Drill

George Mikan improved his shooting skills by practicing shooting with both hands. Many teams still use the "Mikan drill" today. This drill entails making a **layup** under the basket with the right hand, rebounding, and then quickly repeating the process with the left hand.

Center Bill Russell led the Boston Celtics to 11 championships in 13 seasons. Russell's strong defense and rebounding skills were the "centerpiece" of a team that was nearly unstoppable in the 1950s and 1960s. Russell's teammates often used what they called the "Hey Bill Defense." A player who needed help guarding an **opponent** just called "Hey Bill!" and Russell hurried over to help out.

Russell's championship greatness was recognized in 2009 when the NBA named the Finals MVP trophy after him.

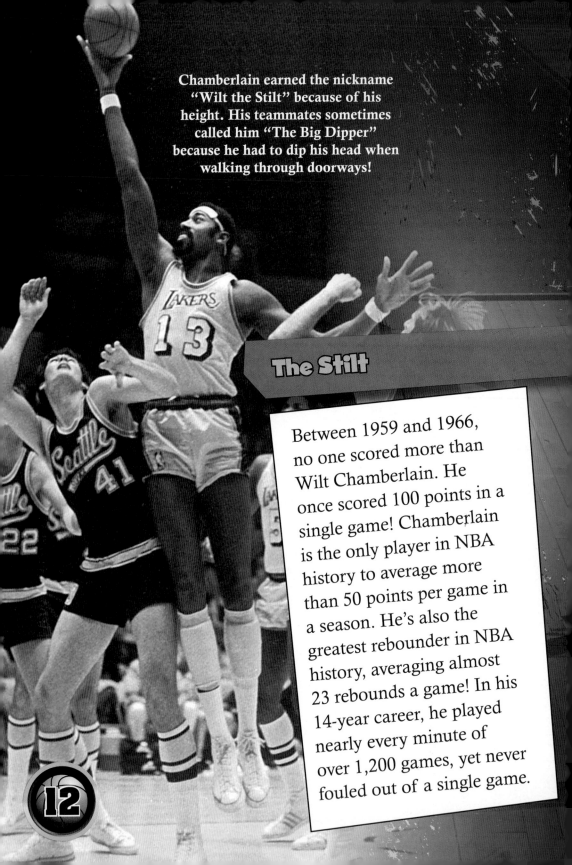

Chamberlain earned the nickname "Wilt the Stilt" because of his height. His teammates sometimes called him "The Big Dipper" because he had to dip his head when walking through doorways!

The Stilt

Between 1959 and 1966, no one scored more than Wilt Chamberlain. He once scored 100 points in a single game! Chamberlain is the only player in NBA history to average more than 50 points per game in a season. He's also the greatest rebounder in NBA history, averaging almost 23 rebounds a game! In his 14-year career, he played nearly every minute of over 1,200 games, yet never fouled out of a single game.

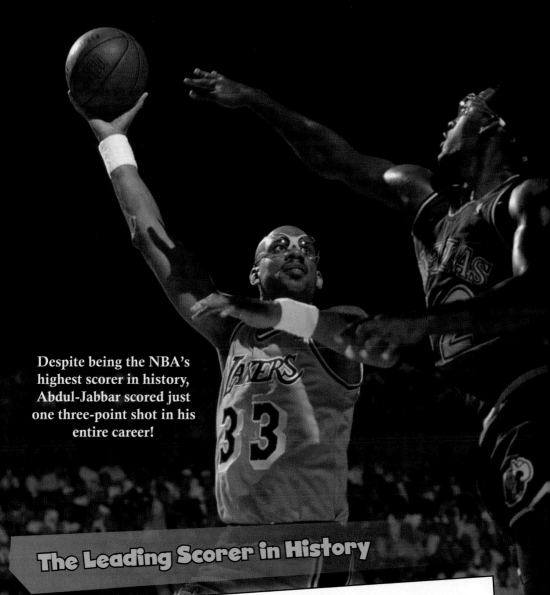

Despite being the NBA's highest scorer in history, Abdul-Jabbar scored just one three-point shot in his entire career!

The Leading Scorer in History

By averaging 24.6 points per game for 2 decades, Kareem Abdul-Jabbar became basketball's all-time leading scorer. During the 1970s and 1980s, Abdul-Jabbar scored a total of 38,387 points for the Milwaukee Bucks and Los Angeles Lakers. His "sky hook" shot and sport goggles became symbols of the sport. For his final game, nearly every player on both sides wore goggles and attempted a sky hook at least once.

13

The Admiral

David Robinson of the San Antonio Spurs led the NBA in rebounding, scoring, free throws, and blocked shots—although not all in the same year. Robinson is one of only four players to get a **quadruple-double** by getting 10 blocks, 10 **assists**, 10 rebounds, and 34 points all in one game. He earned the nickname "the Admiral" because he'd been an officer in the U.S. Navy before he played pro basketball. His first year in the league, 1989, he was voted Rookie of the Year. His last year, 2003, he was an NBA champion.

David Robinson

Leader in "Self Assists"

Moses Malone had a unique way of scoring. He would shoot, miss the basket, grab his own rebound, and then score with it. It was a play that only worked because Malone was the greatest offensive rebounder ever. He led the NBA and **ABA** in offensive rebounds for nine seasons and total rebounds for five seasons. Malone's many rebounds helped him to score 29,580 career points.

14

People often wondered how someone as big as Hakeem "the Dream" Olajuwon could be so fast. The all-time leading shot blocker seemed to appear out of nowhere to swat the ball away or steal it. His "dream shake" move near the basket had defenders going one way while he went the other to score. His defensive skills and point totals made the Houston Rockets back-to-back champions in 1994 and 1995.

Olajuwon was a member of the 1996 men's Olympic basketball team—known as "the Dream Team." He helped the team win a gold medal.

03 How to Play Center

Centers are often the biggest and tallest players on the court. However, being big isn't the only requirement for playing center. Here are the skills that make the best centers stand tall.

Center Stage

The center position earned its name because centers are placed in the middle of a team's other players during play. The forwards are the front line; they move toward the basket to rebound or score up close. The guards play farther from the basket to shoot from the outside and defend against **fast breaks** by the other team. The center stays between those groups and plays where he's needed.

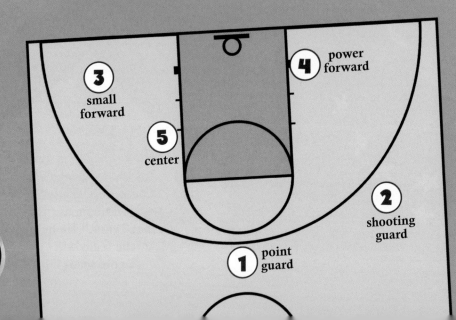

3 small forward

4 power forward

5 center

2 shooting guard

1 point guard

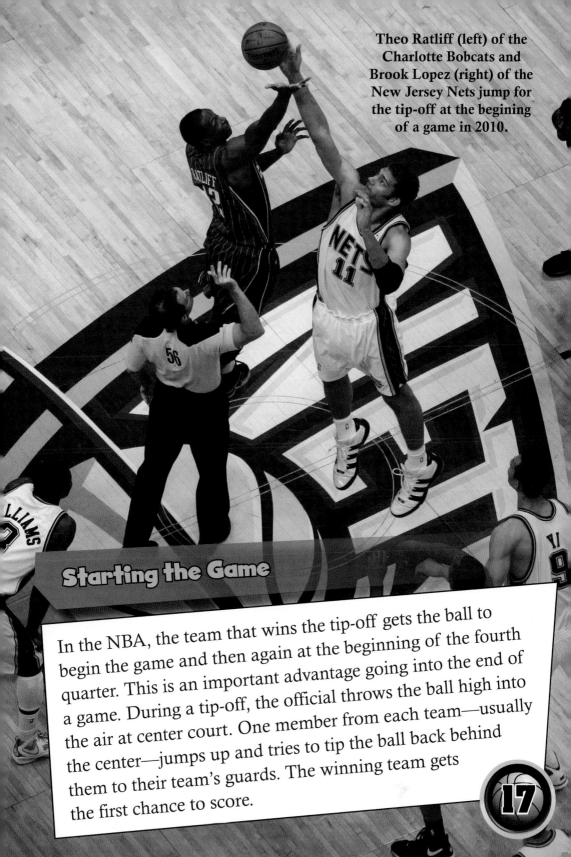

Theo Ratliff (left) of the Charlotte Bobcats and Brook Lopez (right) of the New Jersey Nets jump for the tip-off at the begining of a game in 2010.

Starting the Game

In the NBA, the team that wins the tip-off gets the ball to begin the game and then again at the beginning of the fourth quarter. This is an important advantage going into the end of a game. During a tip-off, the official throws the ball high into the air at center court. One member from each team—usually the center—jumps up and tries to tip the ball back behind them to their team's guards. The winning team gets the first chance to score.

The Center on Offense

Playing center means being active on offense. Centers have to shift around to be ready for a pass and open up scoring chances.

In the Lane

Centers are most effective in the free-throw lane. Unfortunately, players can only stand there for a few seconds at a time. To keep from getting a foul, centers need to move in and out of the painted area or cross over it quickly. Centers need to drive into the lane, look for a pass, and move out again if one isn't coming.

Center Marcus Camby of the Portland Trail Blazers leaps for a rebound "in the paint."

18

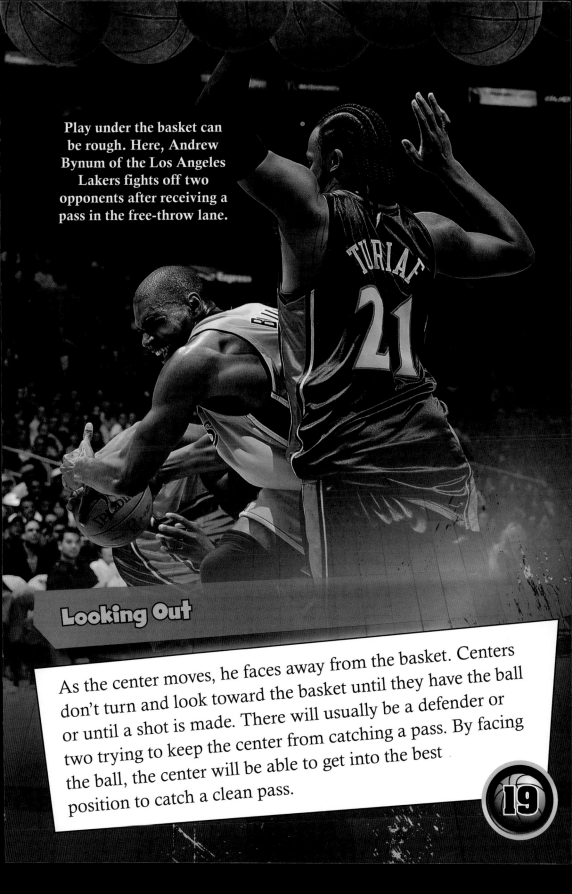

Play under the basket can be rough. Here, Andrew Bynum of the Los Angeles Lakers fights off two opponents after receiving a pass in the free-throw lane.

Looking Out

As the center moves, he faces away from the basket. Centers don't turn and look toward the basket until they have the ball or until a shot is made. There will usually be a defender or two trying to keep the center from catching a pass. By facing the ball, the center will be able to get into the best position to catch a clean pass.

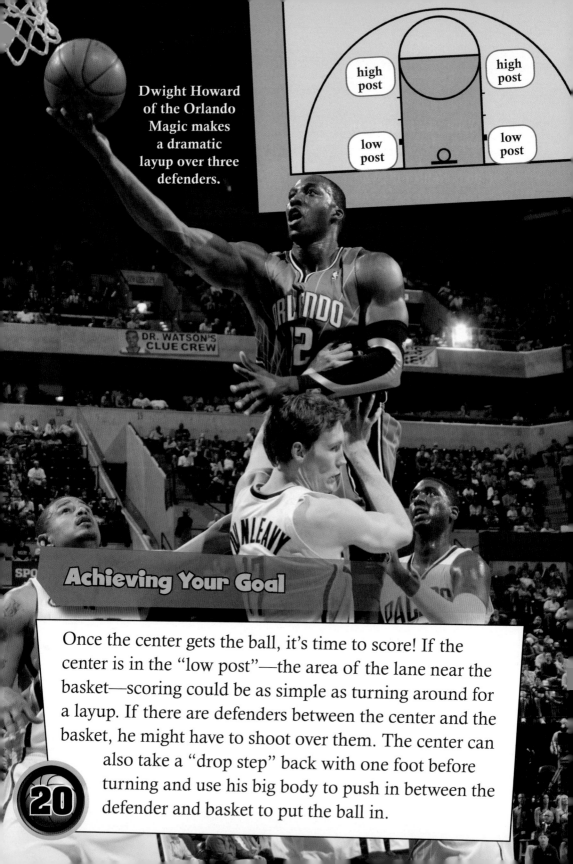

Dwight Howard of the Orlando Magic makes a dramatic layup over three defenders.

high post

high post

low post

low post

DR. WATSON'S CLUE CREW

Achieving Your Goal

Once the center gets the ball, it's time to score! If the center is in the "low post"—the area of the lane near the basket—scoring could be as simple as turning around for a layup. If there are defenders between the center and the basket, he might have to shoot over them. The center can also take a "drop step" back with one foot before turning and use his big body to push in between the defender and basket to put the ball in.

The Denver Nuggets' center Nenê (nuh-NAY) lowers his shoulder and dribbles in close to the basket against Pau Gasol of the Los Angeles Lakers.

Move It or Lose It

If the center gets the ball in the "high post" area near the free-throw line and has a good turnaround jump shot or hook shot, he can shoot from there. If not, he must power his way to the basket. The center turns his inside shoulder toward defenders and **dribbles** with his outside hand. Centers shouldn't dribble the ball more than once or twice before shooting so defenders can't steal the ball.

Share the Glory

If the center isn't able to make a shot after a couple steps, it's better to pass the ball. This is especially true if the center is being **double-teamed**. If more than one defender is guarding the center, one of his teammates will be open. The center has to find the open man and pass the ball to him. Often, the teammate is free to set up a new play or make a basket, which gives the center an assist.

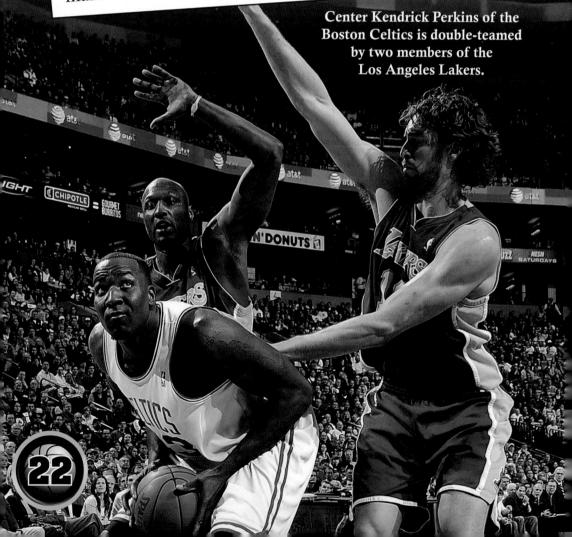

Center Kendrick Perkins of the Boston Celtics is double-teamed by two members of the Los Angeles Lakers.

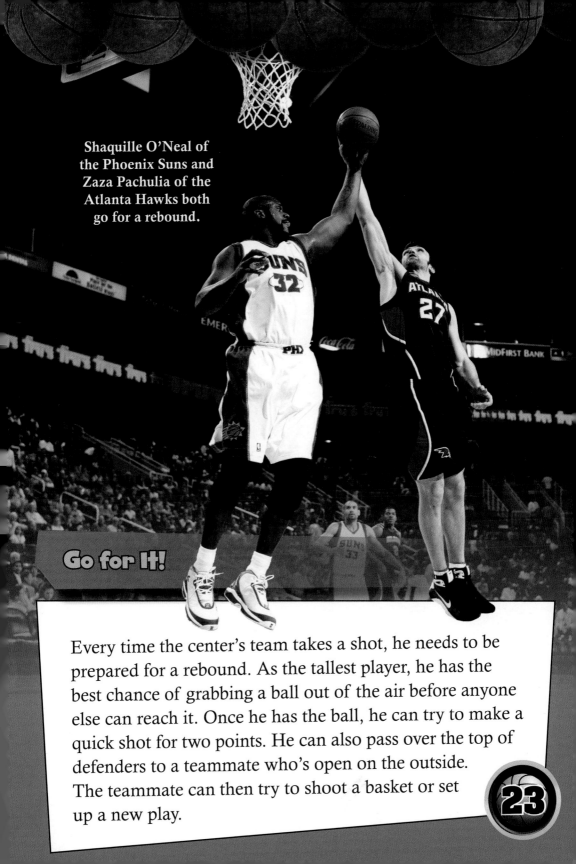

Shaquille O'Neal of the Phoenix Suns and Zaza Pachulia of the Atlanta Hawks both go for a rebound.

Go for It!

Every time the center's team takes a shot, he needs to be prepared for a rebound. As the tallest player, he has the best chance of grabbing a ball out of the air before anyone else can reach it. Once he has the ball, he can try to make a quick shot for two points. He can also pass over the top of defenders to a teammate who's open on the outside. The teammate can then try to shoot a basket or set up a new play.

23

The Center on Defense

On defense, the center needs to keep the other team from doing what he's been doing: scoring up close!

Blocks

Shot blocking is an important skill for centers. By rule, shots can only be blocked when the ball is going up. A center must use height and timing to make a good jump that lets him knock a ball away after it's left the shooter's hand. If he can, the center tips the ball to a teammate so their team can get back on offense quickly.

The New Jersey Nets' Brook Lopez blocks a shot by Dahntay Jones of the Indiana Pacers.

Centers can use their long arms to prevent inside players from receiving passes. A center imagines the path a pass will take to the player he's guarding and gets his hands in that path. Reaching high shuts down overhead passes, and reaching out cuts off incoming passes down low. If a center guards too closely by reaching near his opponent's body, he risks fouling the opponent by touching him.

As Eric Maynor, point guard for the Oklahoma City Thunder, drives to the basket, Minnesota Timberwolves center Al Jefferson keeps his hands up to defend against the pass.

25

Key Skills

Centers use their big bodies to their full advantage. Here's what big men do to create big opportunities.

Body Control

Centers need to move around a lot. They use their big bodies to set up **screens**. If the center knows he won't be shooting, he can cross in front of an opponent who's defending a teammate. Standing in the path of a defender forces the defender to go around to keep guarding. This gives the teammate enough time to shoot or pass without a defender bothering him.

Yao Ming (left) of the Houston Rockets screens the opponent, which allows his teammate Kyle Lowry to drive to the basket.

Stopping a center from scoring up close can be nearly impossible for a smaller defender. Many times, the defender will end up fouling the center while trying to get the ball. A center needs to be a dependable free-throw shooter or he will waste his team's scoring opportunity. Sometimes a team will foul a center who's bad at free throws on purpose because he's unlikely to get two points from the free-throw line.

The Phoenix Suns' Amar'e Stoudemire shoots a free throw.

27

Tim Duncan of the San Antonio Spurs leaps high and dunks the ball in a game against the Atlanta Hawks.

Jump and Reach

A center needs to be a good jumper. He'll have to jump high for the ball numerous times in a game during tip-offs, jump balls, blocks, and rebounds. The higher he jumps, the better his chances of getting the ball and scoring points. Good timing helps, but more often than not a center simply has to be the first player to leave his feet to get the ball. Quick reflexes are the key to making a fast jump.

Shutting Down the Rebound

During rebounds, centers can help their team even when they aren't in position to get the ball. When a forward is rebounding, the center can help by stopping the opponent who shot the ball from getting the rebound. With his back to the basket, the center watches the shooter's eyes and body as he completes the shot to see which way he'll go. The center can then step in the shooter's path and keep him from getting to the basket. This gives his teammates a better chance to catch the rebound.

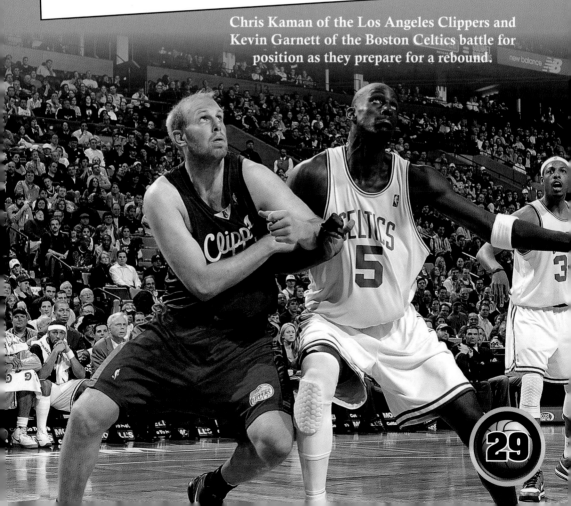

Chris Kaman of the Los Angeles Clippers and Kevin Garnett of the Boston Celtics battle for position as they prepare for a rebound.

29

Box Out

"Boxing out" means using your body to prevent an opponent from getting into position to retrieve a rebound. During an offensive rebound, the center must find either the tallest opponent or the opponent nearest the basket and get between him and the basket as soon as a shot goes up. The center can then use his body to keep the opponent from moving to the area where the ball will come down. During a defensive rebound, the center should box out an opponent waiting near the basket or even the shooter moving in to get his own rebound.

The New York Knicks center David Lee uses his body to box out his opponent and stop him from getting a rebound.

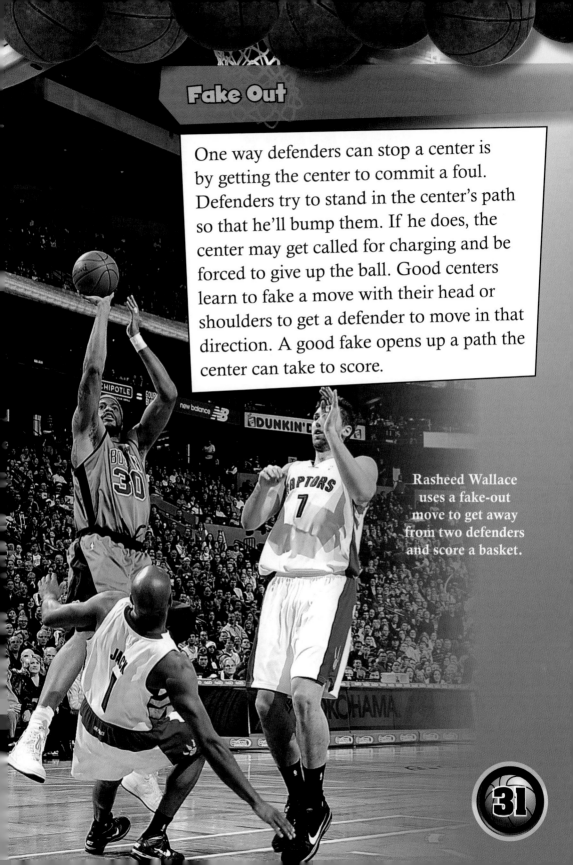

Fake Out

One way defenders can stop a center is by getting the center to commit a foul. Defenders try to stand in the center's path so that he'll bump them. If he does, the center may get called for charging and be forced to give up the ball. Good centers learn to fake a move with their head or shoulders to get a defender to move in that direction. A good fake opens up a path the center can take to score.

Rasheed Wallace uses a fake-out move to get away from two defenders and score a basket.

Getting Ready to Play

Centers need to work their heads as well as their feet. Regular practice, studying plays, and learning an opponent's strengths and weaknesses can give the center an edge during a game.

The Playbook

Action on the court is so fast paced that it may seem as if there's no game plan. However, good offenses start with a plan and stick to it. The center needs to understand his coach's plays so he knows whether to get open or help a teammate on offense. Even when the ball isn't going to the center, his movements should suggest that it is. This helps draw defenders away from the real shooter. It also makes the center's screens more surprising and effective.

Slam dunk! Emeka Okafor of the New Orleans Hornets scores two points after a well-executed play.

The center has to know the best scorers on the other team. If these scorers are "inside" players, the center must be ready to cut off passes to the inside or get between them and the basket so they can't get easy points. If the scorers are "outside" shooters, the center must be willing to move away from the basket so he's in position to cover them and block their shots.

Pau Gasol of the Los Angeles Lakers uses his size to keep his opponent trapped on the outside.

04 Today's Leading Centers

Centers in the NBA today are usually the most electrifying players to watch. They're always in the middle of the most exciting plays. Here's a look at several of the NBA's best modern centers.

Superman

Shaquille O'Neal is the only person named to the NBA's 50 Greatest Players in NBA History who's still playing basketball. O'Neal has combined a high scoring percentage from the field with thousands of free throws for over 28,000 points. He averages 11 rebounds a game, is a four-time NBA champion, and has been named Finals MVP three times.

Hack a Shaq

O'Neal is so unstoppable that teams foul him on purpose before he can shoot. They hope Shaq will miss his free throws and get fewer points. However, it usually just means Shaq scores 25 points instead of 35, which is still impressive.

When a foot injury forced Yao Ming to sit out the 2009–2010 season, Houston fans felt the pain. The Rockets' center had been averaging more than nine rebounds and over 19 points a game. When healthy, the league's tallest player easily shoots over opponents. On defense, he blocks shots and grabs rebounds with ease before making accurate passes to his teammates.

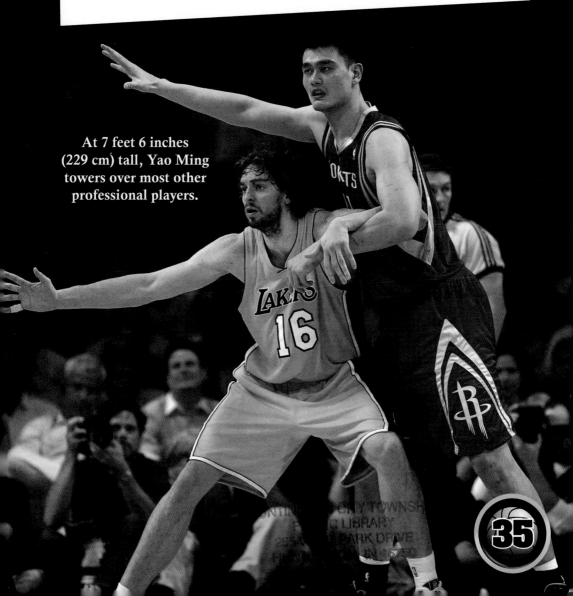

At 7 feet 6 inches (229 cm) tall, Yao Ming towers over most other professional players.

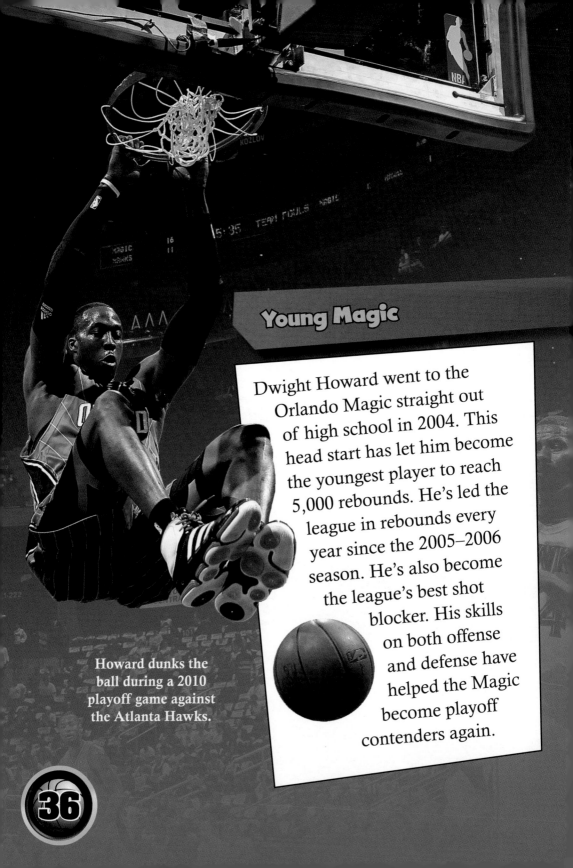

Dwight Howard went to the Orlando Magic straight out of high school in 2004. This head start has let him become the youngest player to reach 5,000 rebounds. He's led the league in rebounds every year since the 2005–2006 season. He's also become the league's best shot blocker. His skills on both offense and defense have helped the Magic become playoff contenders again.

Howard dunks the ball during a 2010 playoff game against the Atlanta Hawks.

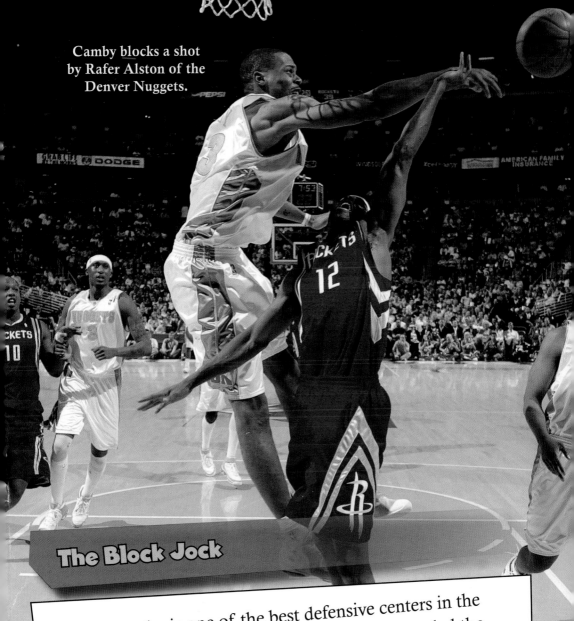

Camby blocks a shot by Rafer Alston of the Denver Nuggets.

The Block Jock

Marcus Camby is one of the best defensive centers in the game today. He's perfected the shot block and has led the league in blocks three times. Camby has averaged over three blocks a game for four seasons. When shots do get by, Camby is also a great defensive rebounder. He's won three out of every 10 rebounds he's gone for on defense since 2004.

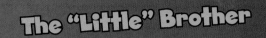

The "Little" Brother

In June 2007, the Los Angeles Lakers chose young Spanish center Marc Gasol for their team. Then in January 2008—before Marc even played for the Lakers—they traded him to the Memphis Grizzlies for Pau Gasol. This is the only time in NBA history that one brother has been traded for another! The Grizzlies got an accurate shooter in Marc. In his first year, he set a **franchise** rookie record for field-goal percentage. He continues to put in five or six baskets a night. While only in the NBA since 2008, his performance on Spanish teams suggests big things for the "little" brother.

In 2008, Marc Gasol was named MVP of the ACM—Spain's pro basketball league.

38

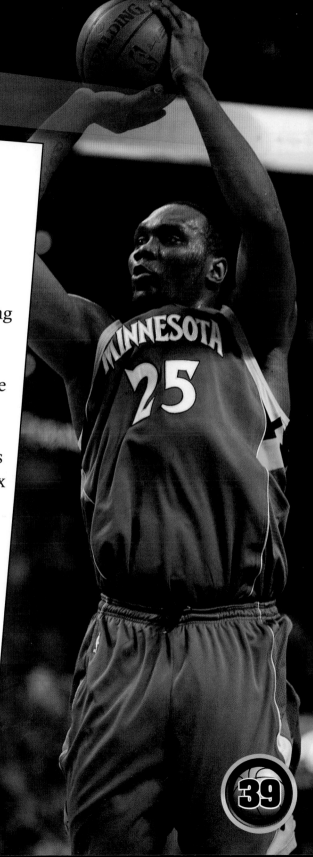

Basketball fans might not always notice a good player on a struggling team, but Al Jefferson deserves some attention. While the Minnesota Timberwolves were among the lowest-scoring teams during the 2007–2008 season, Jefferson made the fourth-highest number of field goals in the league. He's averaged 11 rebounds per game in three of his six seasons since 2004. In a game against the Houston Rockets on January 13, 2010, Jefferson had 26 rebounds—a single-game franchise record!

Jefferson takes a shot during a game against the Boston Celtics in 2009.

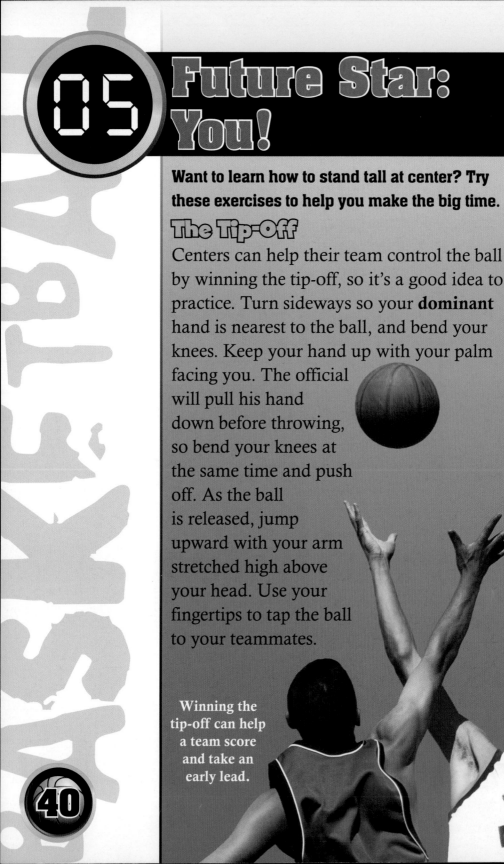

Future Star: You!

Want to learn how to stand tall at center? Try these exercises to help you make the big time.

The Tip-Off

Centers can help their team control the ball by winning the tip-off, so it's a good idea to practice. Turn sideways so your **dominant** hand is nearest to the ball, and bend your knees. Keep your hand up with your palm facing you. The official will pull his hand down before throwing, so bend your knees at the same time and push off. As the ball is released, jump upward with your arm stretched high above your head. Use your fingertips to tap the ball to your teammates.

Winning the tip-off can help a team score and take an early lead.

Start practicing your
jump now. Someday,
you may be able to dunk
like the pros!

Get Up!

Centers must be good jumpers.
To improve your jumping,
practice by facing a wall with
your arms extended above
your head. Use just your legs
to jump as high as you can.
Tap both hands on the wall at
the top of the jump. Have an
adult mark your highest jump
with a piece of tape. Keep
jumping and work on getting
above that mark. This exercise
helps you jump straighter and
trains you to use your legs
when jumping for rebounds.

The Mikan drill develops the quickness and accuracy needed to be good at layups and rebounding.

The Mikan Drill

Start underneath but slightly to the right of the basket. Jump up and shoot a layup on the right side with your right hand. Try to bounce the ball off the backboard and through the net without hitting the rim. Catch the ball with both hands and hold it near your chin while stepping to the other side. Now put in a layup on the left side with the left hand. Do as many layups as you can in one minute, changing sides each time. Try not to let the ball hit the ground.

The Drop Step

A drop step allows centers to take a pass under the net, spin around a defender, and make a quick basket. Have a friend or coach stand in the **wing** and pass the ball to you as you cross the lane to the low post nearest them. Jump to the ball as you catch it and land on both feet. Step back with one foot, turn in that direction so you're facing the basket, and shoot. Work on dropping back using one foot and then the other, as well as starting on both sides of the lane. Next, have a friend stand behind you—between you and the basket—to give you a better idea of how the drop step allows centers to get around a defender.

The drop step is an important move for centers who play close to the basket.

Record Book

Centers need to excel close to the basket. A center who can block and rebound well can lead his team to victory. Let's take a look at the record book to see which centers have dominated those categories.

Career Blocks by a Center:

1. Hakeem Olajuwon   **3,830**
2. Dikembe Mutombo   **3,289**
3. Kareem Abdul-Jabbar   **3,189**
4. Artis Gilmore   **3,178**
5. Mark Eaton   **3,064**

Shaquille O'Neal

Single-Season Blocks by a Center:

1. Mark Eaton	**456**	1984–1985
2. Artis Gilmore	**422**	1971–1972
3. Manute Bol	**397**	1985–1986
4. Elmore Smith	**393**	1973–1974
5. Hakeem Olajuwon	**376**	1989–1990

Single-Game Blocks by a Center:

1. Shaquille O'Neal (still active)	**15**	11/20/1993
Manute Bol	**15**	02/26/1987
3. Mark Eaton	**14**	02/18/1989
4. Shawn Bradley	**13**	04/07/1998
Manute Bol	**13**	02/02/1990
Manute Bol	**13**	03/21/1989

Career Rebounds by a Center:

1. Wilt Chamberlain   **23,924**
2. Bill Russell   **21,620**
3. Moses Malone   **17,834**
4. Kareem Abdul-Jabbar   **17,440**
5. Artis Gilmore   **16,330**

Single-Season Rebounds by a Center:

1. Wilt Chamberlain   **2,149**   1960–1961
2. Wilt Chamberlain   **2,052**   1961–1962
3. Wilt Chamberlain   **1,957**   1966–1967
4. Wilt Chamberlain   **1,952**   1967–1968
5. Wilt Chamberlain   **1,946**   1962–1963

Artis Gilmore

All-Star Game Appearances by a Center:

1. Kareem Abdul-Jabbar   19
2. Shaquille O'Neal (still active)   15
3. Wilt Chamberlain   13
4. Moses Malone   12
    Hakeem Olajuwon   12
    Bill Russell   12

Glossary

ABA: American Basketball Association, a professional basketball league that existed from 1967 to 1976

assist: when a player makes a pass that enables a teammate to score

defense: the team trying to stop the other team from scoring

dominant: the stronger one with more control

double-team: when two people defend against a single player

dribble: to move around the court while bouncing the ball on the floor

dunk: to throw the basketball into the basket from above the rim

fast break: when a team gets the ball and takes it quickly back the other way for a shot up close against little defense

field goal: a basket scored on any shot except for a free throw

foul: to break the rules, often to try to keep a player from scoring

franchise: a professional sports team that is a member of an organized league

free throw: a chance to shoot for one point after being fouled; the shot is made from a line in front of the basket with no defenders

hook shot: a shot made over the head with the hand that is farther from the basket

layup: a shot made from beneath the basket by bouncing the ball off the backboard and into the net

NBA: National Basketball Association, the men's professional basketball league in the United States; the NBA also includes the Toronto (Canada) Raptors

offense: the team trying to score

opponent: the person or team you must beat to win a game

quadruple-double: getting 10 or more of four of the following in a single game: points, assists, blocks, steals, or rebounds

rebound: to recover a ball off a missed shot

screen: a play where one player moves to block a defender to give a teammate a chance to get open for a pass

shot clock: a timer that counts down how long an offense has before it must shoot the ball

wing: a spot where the free-throw line would cross over the three-point line if the free-throw line were extended

Books

Bowen, Fred. *Off the Rim.* Atlanta, GA: Peachtree Publishers, 2009.

Christopher, Matt. *Shoot for the Hoop.* Chicago, IL: Norwood House Press, 2009.

Doeden, Matt. *The World's Greatest Basketball Players.* Mankato, MN: Capstone Press, 2010.

Hafer, Todd. *Three-Point Play.* Grand Rapids, MI: Zonderkidz, 2005.

Schaller, Bob, and Dave Harnish. *The Everything Kids' Basketball Book.* Avon, MA: Adams Media, 2009.

Slade, Suzanne. *Basketball: How It Works.* Mankato, MN: Capstone Press, 2010.

Web Sites

www.hoophall.com
Learn about the history of basketball at the online version of the Naismith Memorial Basketball Hall of Fame. Read the biographies of the greatest basketball players of all time.

www.nba.com
The official Web site of the National Basketball Association has information about teams and players both current and historic. Fans can see video, get news, check scores, and look over game or season statistics.

www.nba.com/kids
The NBA's official Web page for kids lets you play games, join fan clubs for your favorite team, and learn exercises to make you a better basketball player.

www.sikids.com/basketball/nba
The *Sports Illustrated* Web page for kids lets you follow your favorite NBA team. On this site, you'll find scores and news updates about your favorite sport.

Index

About the Author

Jason Glaser is a freelance writer and stay-at-home father living in Mankato, Minnesota. He has written over fifty nonfiction books for children, including books on sports stars such as Tim Duncan. When he isn't listening to sports radio or writing, Jason likes to play volleyball and put idealized versions of himself into sports video games.